DISNEY · PIXAR

THE GOOD DINOSAUR

CRASH, BOOM, ROAR!

By Susan Amerikaner

Illustrated by the Disney Storybook Art Team

Random House 🏠 New York

Poppa hears a sound.

What is it?

Dear Parents:

Congratulations! Your child is taking the first steps on an exciting journey. The destination? Independent reading!

STEP INTO READING® will help your child get there. The program offers five steps to reading success. Each step includes fun stories and colorful art or photographs. In addition to original fiction and books with favorite characters, there are Step into Reading Non-Fiction Readers, Phonics Readers and Boxed Sets, Sticker Readers, and Comic Readers—a complete literacy program with something to interest every child.

Learning to Read, Step by Step!

Ready to Read Preschool–Kindergarten
• big type and easy words • rhyme and rhythm • picture clues
For children who know the alphabet and are eager to begin reading.

Reading with Help Preschool–Grade 1
• basic vocabulary • short sentences • simple stories
For children who recognize familiar words and sound out new words with help.

Reading on Your Own Grades 1–3
• engaging characters • easy-to-follow plots • popular topics
For children who are ready to read on their own.

Reading Paragraphs Grades 2–3
• challenging vocabulary • short paragraphs • exciting stories
For newly independent readers who read simple sentences with confidence.

Ready for Chapters Grades 2–4
• chapters • longer paragraphs • full-color art
For children who want to take the plunge into chapter books but still like colorful pictures.

STEP INTO READING® is designed to give every child a successful reading experience. The grade levels are only guides; children will progress through the steps at their own speed, developing confidence in their reading.

Remember, a lifetime love of reading starts with a single step!

Published in the United States by Random House Children's Books, a division of Penguin
Random House LLC, 1745 Broadway, New York, NY 10019, and in Canada by Random House
of Canada, a division of Penguin Random House Ltd., Toronto, in conjunction with Disney
Enterprises, Inc.

Step into Reading, Random House, and the Random House colophon are registered trademarks of
Penguin Random House LLC.

Visit us on the Web!
StepIntoReading.com
randomhousekids.com

Educators and librarians, for a variety of teaching tools, visit us at RHTeachersLibrarians.com

ISBN 978-0-7364-3367-9 (trade) — ISBN 978-0-7364-8200-4 (lib. bdg.) —
ISBN 978-0-7364-3368-6 (ebook)

Printed in the United States of America   10 9 8 7 6

Crack. Crack! CRACK!

It is Arlo!

Arlo hears the river.

Burble. Bubble. Gurgle!

Arlo hears a storm.

Crash. Boom. Bang!

Spot and Arlo howl.

<u>Yoooooowwww!</u>

Arlo and Spot play.

Animals pop up.

<u>Pop.</u> <u>Pop!</u> <u>POP!</u>

A T. rex <u>ROARS</u>!

Spot bites.

Arlo yells.

Owwww!

OUCH!

Arlo hears a fire.

Hiss. Crackle. Snap!

Arlo hears Momma.

<u>ARLO!</u>

Momma hears Arlo.

<u>MOMMA!</u>

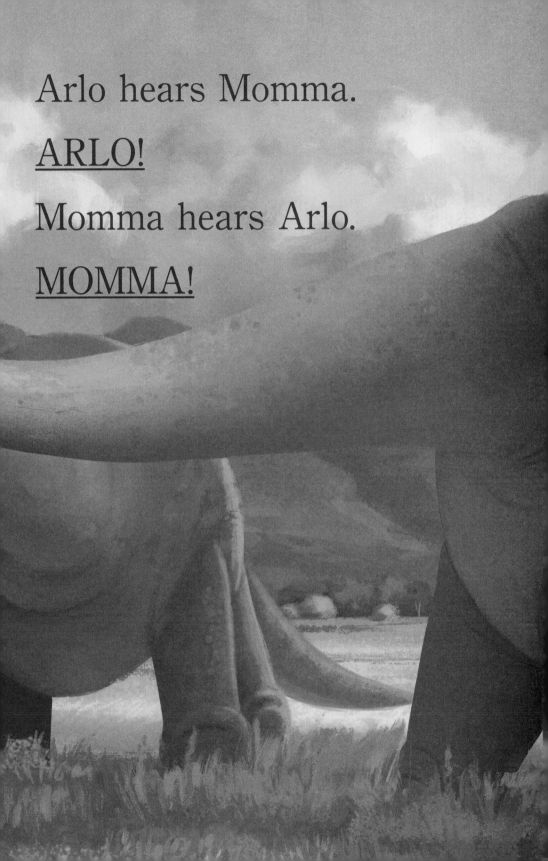

The sound of home
is the best sound of all!